T0365617

Dreams

Written by
Edmond Hartnett

Illustrated by Anthony Damato

He comes each night when you go to bed.

ч

On his breast you softly nestle your head.

He takes you gently by the hand and whisks
you off to slumber land.

Before you know it you are far away
doing things in a magic kind of way
on a pirate ship far out to sea
doing things that just can't be.

Then you are in a candy store
Eating ice cream, and then more.

Riding in a small canoe
Doing all the things you want to do.

A giant train roars into sight.

15

And you are the engineer tonight
You toot the whistle and clang the bell
Tip your cap "All Aboard" you yell.

Then you are in an amusement park
Riding along alone in the dark.

He goes away with the morning light
But will return to you tonight.

Each of us is blessed with our very own
Who comes to us when we are alone
To show us things we haven't seen
To make us what we might have been.

Order this book online at www.trafford.com
or email orders@trafford.com

Most Trafford titles are also available at major online book retailers.

 www.trafford.com

North America & international
toll-free: 844 688 6899 (USA & Canada)
fax: 812 355 4082

Our mission is to efficiently provide the world's finest, most comprehensive book publishing service, enabling every author to experience success. To find out how to publish your book, your way, and have it available worldwide, visit us online at www.trafford.com

Because of the dynamic nature of the Internet, any web addresses or links contained in this book may have changed since publication and may no longer be valid. The views expressed in this work are solely those of the author and do not necessarily reflect the views of the publisher, and the publisher hereby disclaims any responsibility for them.

ISBN: 978-1-4269-3812-2 (sc)
ISBN: 978-1-4669-2438-3 (e)

Print information available on the last page.

Trafford rev. 06/10/2022

Printed in the United States
by Baker & Taylor Publisher Services

Printed in the United States
by Baker & Taylor Publisher Services